DEAR DIARY, **WOOF!** TODAY I PLAYED OUTSIDE.

IT WAS TUESDAY, SO I DUG UP A STICK AND BARKED AT A BIRD.... BUT THEN I SMELLED SOMETHING NEW.

I FOLLOWED THE SMELL ACROSS TWO BACKYARDS AND DOWN TO A DRAINPIPE.
THE SMELL WASN'T A TREAT. OR A TENNIS BALL. OR AN OLD BOOT...

I FOUND A KITTY!

Troy Cummings

Random House 🏠 New York

DEAR MUSIC TEACHER,

I FOUND A KITTY! CAN YOU HELP HIM?

HIS NAME IS SCAMPER!

I REALLY REALLY REALLY WANT TO KEEP HIM, BUT MY PERSON IS ALLERGIC TO CATS.

ACHOO!

SCAMPER LIKES TO EAT, PLAY, AND POOP IN A BOX. HE ALSO LIKES TO SING! I KNOW HE WOULD MAKE ♪ BEAUTIFUL MUSIC ♪ WITH YOUR STUDENTS.

YOUR NEIGHBOR,

ARFY

Dear Arfy,

Scamper is a wonderful kitten. His tail twitches to the beat!

But his high notes are simply too much.

I'm sorry. I was hoping for more harmony in my household. But with Scamper here, I can hardly find a single measure of rest.

Best wishes in your search,

Maestro Mitch

DEAR CUTE LITTLE
NEIGHBOR BABIES,

I FOUND A KITTY!

HE'S A LOT LIKE YOU. HE TAKES
NAPS, EATS EVERY TWO HOURS,
AND LIKES TO CRAWL UNDER
THE COUCH ON HIS TUMMY.

CAN YOU HELP HIM?

SINCERELY,
ARFY

Dear Arfy,

We have wanted a widdle itty-bitty kitty since the day we were born!

We snuggled with him in the morning, nuzzled with him in the afternoon, and squeezed him like a teddy bear at night.

But then a funny thing happened. He squirmed out of our arms and ran out the door.

Guess we'll go back to snuggling our fuzzy-wuzzy sheep blankie.

Bennie, Bonny, and Boo

DEAR NICE MECHANIC,

CAN YOU HELP MY KITTY?

I SAW A MOUSE AT YOUR GARAGE ONE TIME, AND WE ALL KNOW CATS ARE GREAT AT CHASING MICE!

I'LL BET SCAMPER WOULD POUNCE ON THE CHANCE TO HELP YOU OUT.

YOUR PAL,
ARFY

🔧 LUGNUT GARAGE

Dear Arfy,

You're right. My garage has a HUGE mouse problem. Those little squeakers are bumper-to-bumper in here!

I was all revved up to give Scamper a chance. But he didn't eat a single mouse—he just played with them!

Sorry to throw a wrench in your plans, but I need a mouser who's willing to sink his teeth into his work.

Emily Lugnut
Mechanic

Thank You!

TO THE PEOPLE IN THE FANCY BUILDING
WITH THE RED CARPET OUT FRONT,

CAN YOU HELP MY KITTY?

SCAMPER'S FUR IS SHINY,
AND HIS EYES
ARE SPARKLY-LIKE THE
STARS ON YOUR SIDEWALK.

WOOF ALL DUE RESPECT,

ARFY

⚡ TELEGRAM ⚡

> **TO** Arfy   **FROM** Melissa Glitz, talent agent

Arfy, baby!

I've been on the prowl for someone like Scamper. From the moment he entered my studio, I knew he'd be a superstar.

All I had to do was style his fur. And polish his teeth. And do something about those claws.

But then, right after his photo shoot, Scamper gagged. And twitched. And hacked up a two-pound hair ball. Right into my designer handbag.

So sorry, darling, but our little glamorpuss would be more at home on a living room rug than on the red carpet.

XOXO

Missy

DEAR CAT-LOVER GUY,

I WAS SNIFFING AROUND YOUR BUSHES, AND I NOTICED SOMETHING ABOUT YOUR HOUSE.

YOU HAVE CAT CURTAINS, A CAT CLOCK, CAT WALLPAPER, A CAT SOFA, A CAT TOILET SEAT, AND A WHOLE BUNCH OF TINY SHINY CAT STATUES.

BUT YOU DON'T HAVE AN ACTUAL CAT!

CAN YOU HELP MY KITTY? I THINK SCAMPER WOULD FIT RIGHT IN.

HOPEFULLY,

ARFY

Dear Arfy,

I've spent my whole life collecting kitty-cat knickknacks. Scamper is just what I was missing!

Our first morning together was dreamy. I fed him, brushed him, and tucked him in to his kitty bed. We both purred with delight.

But then he started to play. That frisky kitten knocked over my entire collection of ceramic cats! My figurines—and my heart—were shattered.

I'm sorry, but Scamper is too playful to be part of my collection.

Herbert Delgato

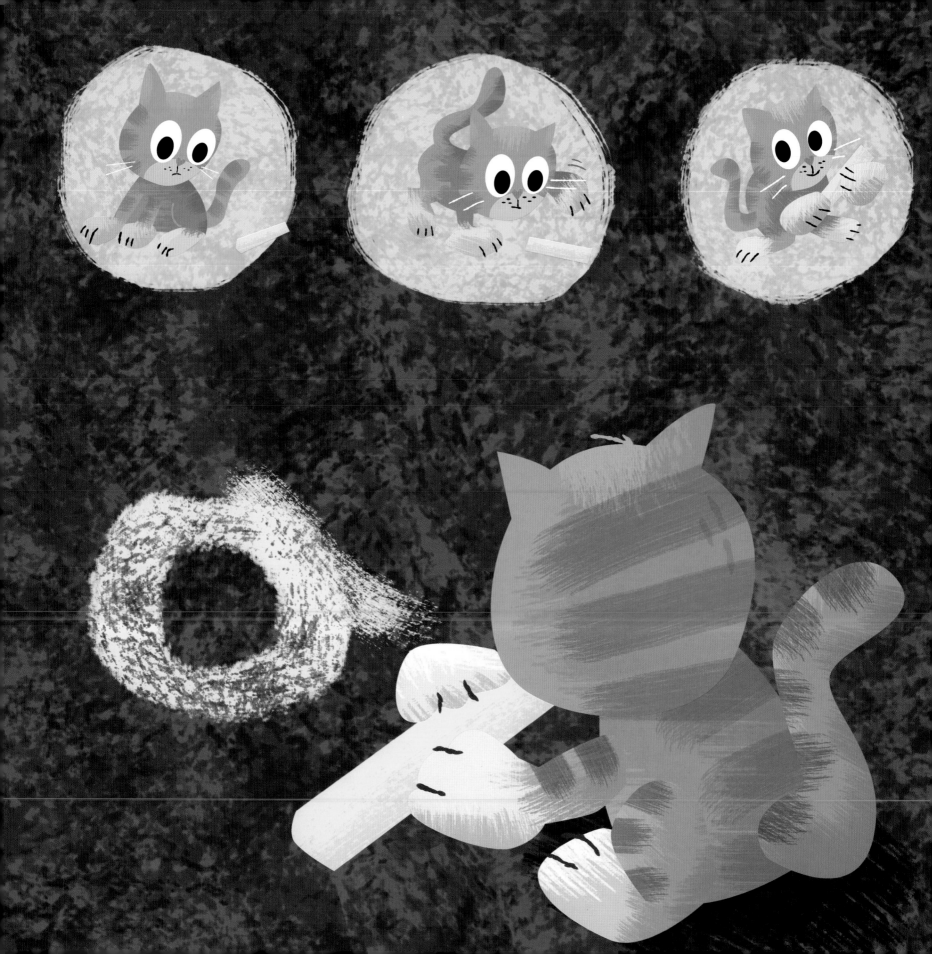

arfy,

don't be sad. you're a goooooood doggy.

thank you for trying to find me a home. i sang! i cuddled! i played! i got brushed!

but...meow do i put this? none of those people were right for me. i need a home where i can do ALL of those things.

but where could we find such a place?

scamper